Same, but Different

Written by Lee-Ann Wright

Look at these animals.
Some animals can look
like other animals,
but they are different.

wet skin

frog

This is a frog.
Look at its skin.
A frog has wet skin.

toad

dry skin

This is a toad.
Look at its skin.
A toad has dry skin.

butterflies

Look at these insects.
They are butterflies
and moths.
Butterflies and moths
can look the same,
but they are different.

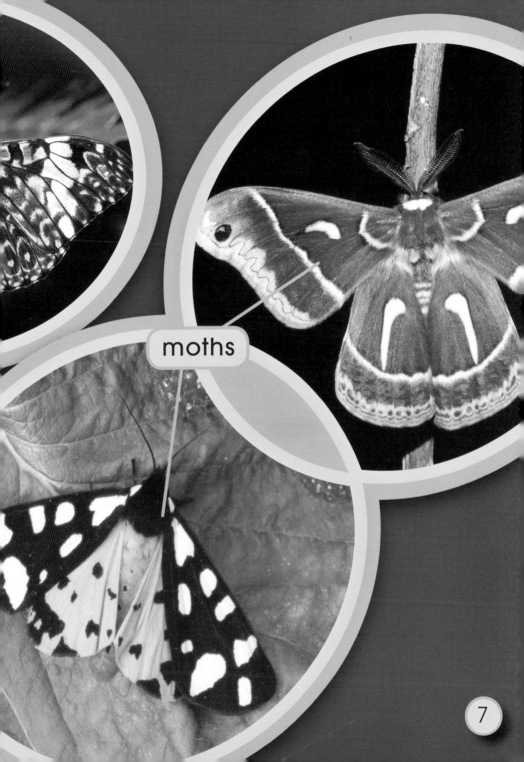

moths

feelers

butterfly

This is a butterfly.
Look at its head.
It has feelers on its head.
There are many butterflies
that fly in the day.

feelers

moth

This is a moth.
It has feelers
on its head, too.
They look like feathers.
There are many moths
that fly at night.

tortoises

Look at these animals.
Some of them are turtles,
and some of them
are tortoises.
Turtles and tortoises
can look the same,
but they are different.

turtles

turtle

flippers

This is a turtle.
A turtle is
good at swimming.
A turtle has
a flat shell and feet
that look like flippers.

tortoise

This is a tortoise.
It has a big shell
and strong legs.
It can't swim,
but it is good at walking.

Some animals can look the same, but they are different.

Comparison chart

Frog		Toad	
	has wet skin		has dry skin

Butterfly		Moth	
	flies in the day		flies at night

Turtle		Tortoise	
	can swim		can't swim

Index

butterfly and moth
. . . . 6, 8-9

frog and toad
. . . . 4-5

turtle and tortoise
. . . . 10, 12-13

Guide Notes

Title: **Same, but Different**

Stage: Early (3) – Blue

Genre: Nonfiction

Approach: Guided Reading

Processes: Thinking Critically, Exploring Language, Processing Information

Written and Visual Focus: Photographs (static images), Index, Labels, Comparison Chart

Word Count: 186

THINKING CRITICALLY
(sample questions)

- Look at the front cover and the title. Ask the children what they know about animals that look the same, but are different.
- Look at the title and read it to the children.
- Focus the children's attention on the index. Ask: "What are you going to find out about in this book?"
- If you want to find out about a turtle and a tortoise, which pages would you look on?
- If you want to find out about a butterfly and a moth, which pages would you look on?
- Look at pages 8 and 9. Why do you think the butterfly has bright colors and the moth has dark colors?
- Look at pages 12 and 13. How do you think having a shell could help the turtle and tortoise?

EXPLORING LANGUAGE

Terminology
Title, cover, photographs, author, photographers

Vocabulary
Interest words: same, different, frog, toad, butterfly, moth, turtle, tortoise, insects, flippers
High-frequency words: other, many
Positional words: on, in
Compound word: butterfly

Print Conventions
Capital letter for sentence beginnings, periods, commas